PRESERVING AND MANUFACTURING SECRETS

All Kinds of Fruits and Vegetables

MAXWELL PRESS

PRESERVING AND MANUFACTURING SECRETS

All Kinds of Fruits and Vegetables

Frank M. Reed

MAXWELL PRESS

Chennai　　　Trichy　　　New Delhi

MAXWELL PRESS

The edition has been published in india by arrangement with Carson Books, UK

ISBN 978-93-90877-22-5 **Maxwell Press**

All rights reserved No. 44, Nallathambi Street,

Printed and bound in India Triplicane, Chennai - 600 005

MJP 993 © Publishers, 2023

Publisher : **C. Janarthanan**

Publisher's Note

The legacy of a country is in its varied cultural heritage, historical literature, developments in the field of economy and science. The top nations in the world are competing in the field of science, economy and literature. This vast legacy has to be conserved and documented so that it can be bestowed to the future generation. The knowledge of this legacy is slowly getting perished in the present generation due to lack of documentation.

Keeping this in mind, the concern with retrospective acquiring of rare books has been accented recently by the burgeoning reprint industry. Maxwell Press is gratified to retrieve the rare collections with a view to bring back those books that were landmarks in their time.

In this effort, a series of rare books would be republished under the banner, "Maxwell Press". The books in the reprint series have been carefully selected for their contemporary usefulness as well as their historical importance within the intellectual. We reconstruct the book with slight enhancements made for better presentation, without affecting the contents of the original edition.

Most of the works selected for republishing covers a huge range of subjects, from history to anthropology. We believe this reprint edition will be a service to the numerous researchers and practitioners active in this fascinating field. We allow readers to experience the wonder of peering into a scholarly work of the highest order and seminal significance.

Maxwell Press

PRESERVING SECRETS.

To Preserve Eggs.—1. For each patent pail full of water put in one pint of fresh slaked lime, and 1 pint of common salt, mix well, fill your barrel about half full of this fluid, then with a dish, let your fresh eggs down into this, and they will settle down right side up with care every time, and we can assure any one who will try it, that they will keep any reasonable length of time without any further care then to keep them covered with the fluid. Eggs may be laid down in this way any time after June.—2. Eggs may be preserved by keeping them buried in salt, or dipping them dur‑ ing two or three seconds in boiling water. The white of the egg then forms a kind of membrane, which envelops the interior, and defends it from the air.—3. The week before going to sea, on a four month's voyage, I gathered in sixty dozen eggs for cabin sea-stores, taking especial pains to prove every egg of the lot a good one; besides, I got them from my farmer friends, and knew they were all fresh. Then I fixed them for keeping, by taking five or six dozen at a time in a basket, and dipping them about five seconds in the cook's "copper" of boiling water. After scalding, I passed the eggs through a bath, made by dissolving about five pounds of the cheapest brown sugar in a gallon of water, and laid them out on the galley floor to dry. Then I had my sixty dozen eggs sugar-coated. I packed them in charcoal dust instead of salt; I tried salt ten years, and I dont believe it preserves eggs a mite. The steward had strict orders to report every bad egg he should find. During the voyage he brought three, not absolutely spoiled, but a little old like. All the others, or what was left of them, were as fresh when we came in as they were when I packed them away.—4. A Parisian paper recommends the following method for the preservation of eggs: Dissolve four ounces of beeswax in eight ounces of warm olive oil, in this put the tip of the finger and anoint the egg all round. The oil will immediately be absorbed, and the shells and pores filled up by the wax. If kept in a cool place the eggs, after two years, will be as good as if fresh laid.—5. Take of quicklime one pound; salt, one pound; saltpetre, three ounces; water one gallon. It is necessary that the solution be boiled ten or fifteen minutes, and when cold put in the eggs, small end downward, using a vessel lined with lead, and placing in a cold but dry cellar.—6. Dip them into a solution of gun-cotton, (collodion), so as to exclude the air from the pores of the shell; or the collodion may be applied with a brush.—7. A writer recommends the dissolving of gum shellac in alcohol, when the mixture may be applied with a common paint-brush. When dry, pack in bran, points downward. Eggs so preserved will keep a very long time. When about to be used, the varnish may be washed off. —8. Get a good sweet wooden box, put about an inch of salt on the bottom; take sweet grease of any kind, lard or drippings, rub the eggs all over with it and put them, the little end down, in the salt; then spread a layer of salt and then add more eggs.—9. Pack the eggs in a cask, with the smaller ends downward; and fill up the cask with melted tallow. This method is practiced very extensively in Russia and in other parts of Europe, and is generally successful. —10. Keep them at the temperature of 40^{v} or less in a refrigerator. Specimens had been exhibited, which were fourteen months old, and still perfectly fresh and sweet.—11. Apply with a brush a solution of gum arabic to the the shells, or immerse the eggs therein; let them dry, and afterwards pack them in dry charcoal dust. This prevents their being affected by any alterations of temperature.— 12. Of all the materials that have been recommended for this purpose, water glass, or silicate of soda, is the most effectual and least objectionable.

To Preserve Apples.—1. By selecting the best of fruit, and carefully enveloping each specimen separately in paper so that the air cannot pass through, the time of keeping in a sound and eatable condition can be greatly prolonged. After covering each apple with paper, select a light wooden box and cover it on the inside, or outside, with paper either before, or after putting in the fruit, as the case may be. Those persons who are desirous of preserving a small quantity of apples will be amply repaid for their trouble by trying the above experiment. The fruit should not be disturbed after packing until the box is opened at the time the fruit is to be eaten. —2. A layer of dry sawdust was sprinkled at the bottom of the box, and then a layer of apples placed in it so that they did not touch each other. Upon these were placed a little layer of sawdust, and so on until the box was filled. The boxes, after being packed in this way, were placed on the wall in the cellar, up from the ground, where they kept, perfectly retaining their freshness and flavor, until brought out.—3. Apples for keeping should be laid out on a dry floor for three weeks. They then may be packed away in layers, with dry straw between them. Each apple should be rubbed with a dry cloth as it is put away. They should be kept in a cool place, but should be sufficiently covered with straw to protect them from frost. They should be plucked on a dry day. They also keep if packed in dry sand.—4. An excellent method for preserving apples through the winter is to put them in barrels or boxes, surrounding each apple with some dry mould or gypsum (plaster of Paris)—not the calcined used for casts, models, etc.—and keep in a dry cool outhouse.

To Preserve Peaches.—Take moderate sized peaches before they are quite ripe, cut a small slit in the end and take out the stone, set them to boil in cold water, and let them remain till about half done, then throw them into an earthen pan containing cold water. The next day put them into a preserving-pan, with as much of the syrup (prepared as above) as will cover them, let them boil for five minutes, then lay them aside till next day in an earthen-ware pan; boil them three days successively in the same syrup, which at the end of that time ought to be rather thicker than honey; if it does not appear to be so, boil it until it is thick enough.

To Preserve Green Grapes.—The grapes must not be too old; the best time is just before the seed begins to harden. They are after being picked and freed from stems, put into bottles (strong wine or champagne bottles are best) so as nearly to fill the latter. These are then filled with fresh and clean water. After this they are all placed in a large kettle, partially filled with cold water, and the temperature raised nearly to the boiling point. The water in the bottles expands by the heat, and part is driven out. As soon as sufficiently heated, they are taken off, enough water poured out of each bottle to merely allow a well-fitting cork to be pressed in tightly. After being corked they are sealed up with sealing-wax or common beeswax. As the bottles cool down a partial vacuum is left in the neck of each. Grapes thus preserved have kept for years in this climate, where canned fruit almost invariably spoils during the hot summers. They can at any time be opened and prepared like fresh grapes, no difference will be found in the taste. It is better to use the water, also, in which they were kept, as it contains a large per centage of tartaric acid, which gives them the pleasant sour taste.

To Preserve Tomatoes.—Take of good ripe tomatoes, such a quantity as you wish to preserve, pare them, cut them in quarters, (if large ones,) place them in a stew pan with a little water, so they will not burn; being a very juicy fruit, they require to be cooked until the juice is nearly all out; then add white sugar—one pound to each pound of fruit; cook slowly one-half hour.

To Preserve Green Peas.—When full grown, but not old, pick and shell the peas. Lay them on dishes or tins in a cool oven, or before a bright fire; do not heap the peas on the dishes, but merely cover them with peas, stir them frequently, and let them dry very gradually. When hard let them cool, then pack them in stone jars, cover close, and keep them in a very dry place. When required for use, soak them for some hours in cold water, till they look plump before boiling; they are excellent for soup.

To Have Green Corn the Year Round.—Gather it with the husks on, put in the bottom of a clean barrel some salt, proceed and fill the barrel as with pork, a layer of corn, then a layer of salt; when full, put on a large stone for pressure, add a little pickle of salt and water. Set the barrel in a cool place in the cellar, do not let it freeze, and it will keep perfect a year or more. When you wish to use it, take of the husks, soak it twenty hours in cold water, boil it and eat. Some days in February you can eat succotash and laugh at the storm. For this purpose, Stowell's Evergreen is best, but any good sweet corn will do. Used in this way, it can be enjoyed, as it is never hurtful.

To Preserve Cherries.—To a pound of cherries, allow three quarters of a pound of fine loaf-sugar; carefully stone them, and as they are done throw part of the sugar over them; boil them fast with the remainder of the sugar, till the fruit is clear and the syrup thick. Take off the scum as it rises.

To Preserve Meat.—Place in large earthenware pans, putting clean heavy stones on it, and covering it with skim milk; the milk will become sour, of course, but may afterward serve as food for pigs, and the meat will be found to have kept its natural primitive freshness, even after eight or ten days. This is a German method, and may answer where the ice house or spring house is wanting, and where the skim milk is plenty.

To Peserve Meat with Phenyl Paper.—This article would be useful for packing meat and other substances liable to decay. It can be prepared by fusing five parts stearie acid at a gentle heat, mixing well with two parts carbolic acid and five parts melted paraffine, and stirring until the whole has become solid, and applying in the same manner as wax paper is made.

To Keep Beans fresh for Winter.—Procure a wide mouthed stone jar, lay on the bottom of it some freshly pulled French beans, and over them put a layer of salt; fill the jar up in this manner with alternate layers of beans and salt. The beans need not all be put in at the same time, but they are better if the salt be put on while they are quite fresh. They will keep good all through the winter. When going to use them, steep for some hours in fresh cold water.

To keep fresh Butter in Summer.—A simple mode of keeping butter in warm weather, where ice is not handy, is to invert a common flower pot over the butter, with some water in the dish in which the butter is laid. The orifice in the bottom may be corked or not. The porousness of the earthenware will keep the butter cool. It will be still cooler if the pot be wrapped with a wet cloth. Not the porosity of the earthenware, but the rapid abstraction of heat by external evaporation causes the butter to become hard.

To keep Suet.—Suet may be kept a year; thus: Choose the firmest and most free from skin or veins, remove all traces of these, put the suet in the saucepan at some distance from the fire, and let it melt gradually; when melted pour it into a pan of cold spring-water; when hard, wipe it dry, fold it in white paper, put it in a linen bag, and keep it in a cool, dry place; when used, it must be scraped, and it will make an exellent crust with or without butter.

Keeping Vegetables.—Sink a barrel two-thirds of its depth into the ground (a box or cask will answer a better purpose); heap the earth around the part projecting out of the ground, with a slope on all sides; place the vegetables that you desire to keep in the vessel; cover the top with a water tight cover; and when winter sets in, throw an armful of straw, hay, or something of that sort, on the barrel. If the bottom is out of the cask or barrel, it will be better. Cabbage, celery, and other vegetables, will keep in this way as fresh as when taken from the ground. The celery should stand nearly perpendicular, celery and earth alternating. Freedom from frost, ease of access, and especially freshness, and freedom from rot, are the advantages claimed.

To keep Grapes.—1. They must not be too ripe. Take off any imperfect grapes from the bunches. On the bottom of a keg put a layer of bran that has been well dried in an oven, or in the sun. On the bran put a layer of grapes, with bran between the bunches, so that they may not be in contact. Proceed in the same way with alternate layers of grapes and bran, till the keg is full; then close the keg so that no air can enter.—2. In a box first lay a paper, then a layer of grapes selecting the best bunches and removing all imperfect grapes, then another paper, then more grapes, and so until the box is full; then cover all with several folds of paper or cloth. Nail on the lid, and set in a cool room where it will not freeze. I use small boxes, so as not to disturb more than I want to use in a week or so. Give each bunch plenty of room so they will not crowd, and don't use newspapers. Some seal the stems with sealing wax and wrap each bunch by itself, but **I** get along without that trouble.   The grapes should be looked to several times during the winter.   Should any mould or decay, they should be removed and the good ones again repacked.   By this means I have had, with my pitcher of cider and basket of apples, my plate of grapes daily, besides distributing some among my friends and the sick of the neighborhood.—3. *(Chinese Method.)*   It consist in cutting a circular piece out of a ripe pumpkin or gourd, making an aperture large enough to admit the hand.   The interior is then completely cleaned out, the ripe grapes are placed inside, and the cover replaced and pressed in firmly.   The pumpkins are then kept in a cool place—and the grapes will be found to retain their freshness for a very long time.   We are told that a very careful selection must be made of the pumpkin, the common field pumpkin, however, being well adapted for the purpose in question.

Keeping Fruit.—Have your cellar or fruit-room neither too dry nor too moist.   This is indispensable.   If moist, your fruit will rot; it dry it will shrink.   If you are incredulous about this, set your fruit in your dwelling-room, or where there is a high, dry temperature.   This will satisfy you as to the shrinking.   Dampen a bin or barrel, and keep so for awhile, (with the fruit in it), and you will need no more urging.   The "course between," as the old adage has it, is the right way.   I know we are apt to have our hobbies and go to extremes.   The course between is not always relished. But facts are facts, and they are not only stubborn, but they will always remain so.   Fruit must be put where there is not sufficient moisture to rot it, as an excess will surely do.   On the other hand, the dry must be avoided, or there will be shrinking and a dry fruit. This is as common an experience as life itself. Open bins, unless the cellar or fruit-room be very damp, will dry the fruit.   This is generally so.   Open barrels are less affected in this way, but still affected.   The best way is to close your barrel after the fruit has passed through it sweating, which it will do in a few days, and leave a small open space, say a couple of apertures accross the head of the barrel, of half an inch or less in diameter.   Or, you are pretty safe (in the case of apples, which are more particularly referred to to head up tight, after the sweating operation has gone through with, and the fruit is again dry.   This we have found eminently successful.   We have found some mold where the barrel was closed as soon as filled, the fruit getting moist, (sweating) and the moisture instead of passing off by the vent, had to be absorbed by the wood of the barrel.   But before this is done mischief will be wrought. Still we have known cases of clear exceptions.   But this will not do; we want cases without exceptions, without doubt; we want to save our fruit beyond peradventure. And we can in the way we have described. As to temperature, this cannot be too low, providing it does not freeze the fruit. And uniformity is almost as important as depression of heat. These two are the vital and important points. Kept at the freezing point, or just out of its range, there will be little change in the fruit, either to rot or to mature. An apple can thus be kept "green" the winter through—for aught we know any apple, but certainly the winter fruit. We have it, therefore, in our power, to ripen or not as we like, and this is quite an advantage; to avail ourselves of it any winter with the greatest of interest, and a most decided advantage. We could not well do without it. We keep cold the one part of our cellar, that containing the spring fruit. Frost sometimes steals upon us, but we permit it to steal gradually out again; for the world we would not hurry it, for that would spoil our fruit. When once frosted we permit it to remain so as long as we can, for that it is a safe keeping so long as it lasts. A little fresh air seems to be a benefit. It is hardly our experience, however, as confined fruit, where the air is not damp or mold infected; where it is pure, some from the slight evaporation of the fruit, particularly apples, have always kept well with us so far as we have experimented. Still we see no harm from a change of atmosphere of our room. We therefore, when the air is not damp, occasionally raise our windows a little, or when the temperature is the same as that of the cellar, or a little lower. Rashness here is fatal. If the air without should be warm and a south wind blow, with the windows raised there will be such a change as will seriously affect the fruit. The cold air will be driven out of the cellar or fruit-room. Rather let the cold air in severely. But uniformity, with a little fresh air occasionally, is what is wanted.

Storeing Potatoes.—Potatoes should not be exposed to the sun and light any more than is necessary to dry them after digging them from the hill. Every ten minutes of such exposure, especially in the sun, injures their edible qualities. The flesh is thus rendered soft, yellowish or greenish, and injured in flavor. Dig them when dry, and put them in a dark cellar immediately and keep them there till wanted for use, and there would not be so much fault found about bad quality. This is also a hint to those grocers and marketmen who keep their potatoes in barrels in the sun—that is, if they wish to furnish their customers with a good article.

To keep Potatoes from Sprouting.—To keep potatoes intended for the use of the table from sprouting until new potatoes grow, take boiling water, pour into a tube, turn in as many potatoes as the water will entirely cover, then pour off all the water, handle the potatoes carefully, laying up in a dry place on boards, only one layer deep, and see if you do not have good potatoes the year round, without hard strings and watery ends caused by growing.

Bacon.—The reputation of the Hampshire bacon is owing entirely to the care with which it is cured. The hogs, which are fatted on peas and barley meal, are kept fasting for twenty-four hours at least before they are killed; they are used as gently as possible in the act of killing, which is done by inserting a long-pointed knife into the main artery which comes from the heart. The hair is burnt off with lighted straw, and the dirty surface of the skin scraped off. The carcass is hung up after the entrails have been removed, and the next day, when the meat has become quite cold, it is cut up into flitches. The spareribs are taken out, and the bloody veins carefully removed; the whole is then covered with salt, with a small quantity of saltpetre mixed with it. Sometimes a little brown sugar is added, which gives a pleasant sweetness to the bacon. The flitches are laid on a low wooden table, which has a small raised border at the lower end. The table slants a little, so as to let the brine run off into a vessel placed under it, by a small opening in the border at the lower end. The flitches are turned up and salted every day; those which were uppermost are put under, and in three weeks they are ready to be hung up to dry. Smoking the bacon is no longer as common as it used to be, as simply drying in the salt is found sufficient to make it keep. Those who from early association like the flavor given by the smoke of wood burn sawdust and shavings in a smothered fire for some time under the flitches. When they are quite dry they are placed on a board rack for the use of the family, or are packed with wheat chaff into chests till they are sold. The pratice of cutting the hogs into pieces and pickling them in a vat, being attended with less trouble, is very generally preferred when there is only a sufficient number of hogs killed to serve the farmer's family; but flitches of bacon well cured are more profitable for sale. Corn-fed bacon is at least equal if not superior to the barley-fed, which is considered the prime article in England.

To Cure Beef.—Cut up the beef, and weigh and bulk it up, sprinkling a little salt over it, and let it lay ten or twelve hours, then pack it down in the barrel. To one hundred pounds of beef take one quart of salt, three and one half pints of molasses, one tablespoonful of saltpetre. Put all this into sufficient water to cover the beef; boil and pickle, and skim off all the scum, and when cold pour it over the beef, and weigh it down. Keep the beef covered with the pickle.

To Cure Hams.—1. Take 2½ pounds sugar, 7 ℔s. coarse salt, 2 oz. saltpetre and 4 gallons water, boil together and put on cool to 100 pounds of meat. Let the meat lie in the pickle eight weeks.

—2. To a cask of hams, say from 25 to 30, after having packed them closely and sprinkled them slightly with salt, I let them lie thus for 3 days; then make a brine sufficient to cover them, by putting salt into clear water, making it strong enough to bear up a sound egg or potato. Then add ½ ℔. of saltpetre, and a gallon of molasses; let them lie in the brine for 6 weeks—they are then exactly right. Then take them up and let them drain; then while damp, rub the flesh side and the end of the leg with finely pulverized black, red, or cayenne pepper; let it be as fine as dust, and dust every part of the flesh side, then hang them up and smoke. You may leave them hanging in the smokehouse or other cool place where the rats cannot reach them, as they are perfectly safe from all insects

To Cure Meat.—To one gallon of water add one and a half pounds of salt, half a pound of sugar, half an ounce of saltpetre; half an ounce of potash. In this ratio the pickle to be increased to any quantity desired. Let these be boiled together until all the dirt from the sugar rises to the top and is skimmed off. Then throw it into a tube to cool, and when cold pour it over your beef or pork, to remain the usual time, say four or five weeks. The meat must be well covered with pickle, and should not be put down for at least two days after killing, during which time it should be slightly sprinkled with powdered saltpetre, which removes all the surface blood, etc., leaving the meat fresh and clean. Some omit boiling the pickle, and find it to answer well; though the operation of boiling purifies the pickle by throwing off the dirt always to be found in salt and sugar. If this recipe is properly tried it will never be abandoned. There is none that surpasses it, if so good.

To Pickle Onions.—Have the onions gathered when quite dry and ripe, and with the fingers take off the thin outside skin, then with a knife remove one more skin, when the onion will look quite clear. Have ready some very dry bottles or jars, and as fast as the onions are peeled put them in. Pour over sufficient cold vinegar to cover them, add two teaspoonfuls of allspice and two teaspoonfuls of black pepper, taking care that each jar has its share of the latter ingredients. Tie down with bladder, and put them in a dry place, and in a fortnight they will be fit for use. This is a most simple receipt, and very delicious, the onions being nice and crisp. They should be eaten within six or eight months after being done, as the onions are liable to become soft.

To Pickle Gherkins.—Steep them in strong brine for a week, then pour it off, heat it to the boiling point, and again pour it on the gherkins; in 24 hours drain the fruit on a sieve, put it into wide-mouthed bottles or jars, fill them up with strong pickling vinegar, boiling hot, bung down immediately, and tie it over with bladder. When cold, dip the corks into melted bottle wax. Spice is usually added to the bottles, or else steeped in the vinegar.

☞ In a similar way are pickled, onions, mushrooms, cucumbers, walnuts, samphires, green gooseberries, cauliflowers, melons, barberries, peaches, lemons, tomatoes, beans, radish pods, codlins, red cabbage, (without salt, and with cold vinegar,) beet-root, (without salting,) garlic, peas, etc., etc., observing that the softer and more delicate articles do not require so long soaking in brine as the harder and coarser kinds, and may be often advantageously pickled by simply pouring very strong pickling vinegar over them, without applying heat.

To Pickle Green Corn.—When the corn is a little past the tenderest roasting ear state, pull it; take off one thickness of the husk, tie the rest of the husk down at the silk end in a close and tight manner; place them in a clean cask or barrel compactly together, and put on brine to cover the same of about two-thirds the strength of meat pickle. When ready to use in winter, soak in cold water over night, and if this does not appear sufficient, change the water and freshen still more.

Mixed Pickles.—Take half a pint of half-grown French beans, as nearly of the same size as possible, a dozen gherkins, each from two to three inches long, a small green cucumber cut into slices about half an inch thick; put these into a pan of brine, strong enough to float an egg. Let them lie for three days, stirring them each day, then place them in an enameled preserving pan, with vine leaves under and over them, pour in the brine in which they have been steeped, and cover them closely to prevent the steam escaping; set them over a slow fire, but do not allow them to boil; when they become a green color, drain them through a sieve and let them remain till the other ingredients are ready. Pull a small white cauliflower into branches, and lay it in strong brine, together with half a pint of onions, the size of marbles, peeled, a dozen fresh chities (scarlet,) or a few scarlet capsicums; let them remain three or four days, then arrange them in pickle bottles with the green pickles already done interpersed in a tasteful manner through them. Boil as much good vinegar as will be sufficient to fill up the bottles, with some whole allspice, white pepper, bruised ginger, mace, mustard seed, and slices of horseradish. When the vinegar tastes very strong of these spices, strain it carefully (unless they have been tied in a bag as already recommended). Let the vinegar stand till cold, then fill the bottles and cork securely.

To Can Tomatoes.—The most thorough and reliable mode of canning tomatoes is as follows: They are just sufficiently steamed, not cooked, to scald or loosen the skin, and are then poured upon tables and the skin removed, care being taken to preserve the tomato in as solid a state as possible. After being peeled, they are placed in large pans, with false bottoms perforated with holes, so as to strain off the liquid that emanates from them. From these pans they are carefully placed by hand into the cans, which are filled as solidly as possible—in other words, all are put in that the can will hold. They are then put through the usual process and hermetically sealed. The cans when opened for use, present the tomato not only like the natural vegetable in taste and color, but also in appearance; and moreover, when sealed, they are warranted to keep in any climate, and when opened, will taste as natural as when just plucked from the vine.

To Can Peaches.—Pare and half your peaches. Pack them as closely as possible in the can without any sugar. When the can is full, pour in sufficient pure cold water to fill all the interstices between the peaches, and reach the brim of the can. Let stand long enough for the water to soak into all the crevices—say six hours—then pour in water to replace what has sunk away. Seal up the can, and all is done. Canned in this way, peaches retain all their freshness and flavor. There will not be enough water in them to render them insipid. If preferred, a cold syrup could be used instead of pure water, but the peaches taste most natural without any sweet.

To Can Fruit.—The principle should be understood, in order to work intelligently. The fruit is preserved by placing it in a vessel from which the external air is entirely excluded. This is effected by surrounding the fruit by liquid, and by the use of heat to rarify and expel the air that may be entangled in the fruit or lodged in its pores. The preservation does not depend upon sugar, though enough of this is used in the liquid which covers the fruit to make it palatable. The heat answers another purpose; it destroys the ferment which fruits naturally contain, and as long as they are kept from contact with the external air they do not decompose. The vessels in which fruits are preserved are tin, glass and earthenware. Tin is used at the factories where large quantities are put up for commerce, but is seldom used in families, as more skill in soldering is required than most persons possess. Besides, the tins are not generally safe to use more than once. Glass is the preferable material, as it is readily cleaned and allows the interior to be frequently inspected. Any kind of bottle or jar that has a mouth wide enough to admit the fruit and that can be securely stopped, positively air-tight—which is much closer than water-tight—will answer. Jars of various patterns and patents are made for the purpose, and are sold at the crockery and grocery stores. These have wide mouths, and a glass or metallic cap which is made to fit very tightly by an India-rubber ring between the metal and the glass. The devices for these caps are numerous, and much ingenuity is displayed in inventing them. We have used several patterns without much difference in success, but have found there was some difference in the facility with which the jars could be opened and closed. The best are those in which atmospheric pressure helps the sealing, and where the sole dependence is not upon screws or clamps. To test a jar, light a slip of paper and hold it within it. The heat of the flame will expand the air and drive out a portion of it. Now put on the cap; when the jar becomes cool the air within will contract, and the pressure of the external air should hold the cover on so firmly that it cannot be pulled off without first letting in air by pressing aside the rubber or by such other means as is provided in the construction of the jar. When regular fruit jars are not used, good corks and cement must be provided. Cement is made by melting 1¼ oz. of tallow with 1 ℔. rosin. The stiffness of the cement may be governed by the use of more or less tallow. After the jar is corked, tie a piece of stout drilling over the mouth. Dip the cloth on the mouth of the jar into the melted cement, rub the cement on the cloth with a stick to break up the bubbles, and leave a close covering. The process. Everything should be in readiness, the jars clean, the covers well fitted, the fruit picked over or otherwise prepared, and cement and corks, if these are used, at hand. The bottles or jars are to receive a very hot liquid, and they must be gradually warmed beforehand, by placing warm water in them, to which boiling water is gradually added. Commence by making a syrup in the proportion of a pound of white sugar to a pint of water, using less sugar if this quantity will make the fruit too sweet. When the syrup boils, add as much fruit as it will cover, let the fruit heat in the syrup gradually, and when it comes to a boil ladle it into the jars, or bottles which have been warmed as above directed. Put in as much fruit as possible, and then add the syrup to fill up all the interstices among the fruit; then put on the cover or insert the stopper as soon as possible. Have a cloth at hand dampened in hot water to wipe the necks of the jars. When one lot has been bottled, proceed with more, adding more sugar and water if more syrup is required. Juice fruits will diminish the syrup much less than others. When the bottles are cold, put them away in a cool, dry, and dark place. Do not tamper with the covers in any way. The bottles should be inspected every day for a week or so, in order to discover if any are imperfect. If fermentation has commenced, bubbles will be seen in the syrup, and the covers will be loosened. If taken at once, the contents may be saved by thoroughly reheating.—Another way is to prepare a syrup and allow it to cool.

Place the fruit in bottles, cover with the syrup and then set the bottles nearly up to their rims in a boiler of cold water. Some wooden slats should be placed at the bottom of the boiler to keep the bottles from contact with it. The water in the boiler is then heated and kept boiling until the fruit in the bottles is thoroughly heated through, when the covers are put on, and the bottles allowed to cool. It is claimed that the flavor of the fruit is better preserved in this way than by the other. What may be Preserved.—All the fruits that are used in their fresh state or for pies, etc., and Rhubarb, or Pie-plant, and Tomatoes. Green Peas, and Corn, cannot be readily preserved in families, as they require special apparatus. Strawberries. Hard-fleshed sour varieties, such as the Wilson, are better than the more delicate kinds. Directions for these, as well as for Raspberries, will be found elsewhere. . Currants need more sugar than the foregoing. Blackberries and Huckleberies are both very satisfactorily preserved, and make capital pies. Cherries and Plums need only picking over. Peaches need peeling and quartering. The skin may be removed from ripe peaches by scalding them in water or weak lye for a few seconds, and then tranferring them to cold water. Some obtain a strong peach flavor by boiling a few peach meats in the syrup. We have had peaches keep three years, and were then better than those sold at the stores. Pears are pared and halved, or quartered, and the core removed. The best, high-flavored and melting varities only should be used. Coarse baking pears are unsatisfactory. Apples. Very few put up these. Try some high-flavored ones, and you will be pleased with them. Quinces. There is a great contrast between quinces preserved in this way and those done up in the old way of pound for pound. They do not become hard, and they remain of a fine light color. Tomatoes require cooking longer than the fruits proper.

Drying Fruit.—When much fruit is dried, it is necessary to have a house for the pupose. Small quantities should be so arranged as to be placed near the kitchen fire when taken in at night or during stormy days. Those who have hot-bed sash, can easily arrange a drying apparatus which will dry rapidly and at the same time keep off insects. A hot-bed frame with a bottom to it, and raised above the ground, makes a capital drying box. The sash should be elevated at one end to allow the moisture to pass off, covering the opening with netting.

To Dry Apples.—The most general method adopted in drying apples is, after they are pared, to cut them in slices, and spread them on cloths, tables, or boards, and dry them out-doors. In clear and dry weather this is, perhaps, the most expeditious and best way; but in cloudy and stormy weather this way is attended with much inconvenience, and sometimes loss, in consequence of the apples rotting before they dry. To some extent they may be dried in this way in the house, though this is attended with much inconvenience. The best method that I have ever used to dry apples is to use frames. These combine the most advantages with the least inconvenience of any way, and can be used with equal advantage either in drying in the house or out in the sun. In pleasant weather the frames can be set out-doors against the side of the building, or any other support, and nights, or cloudy and stormy days, they can be brought into the house, and set against the side of the room near the stove or fire-place. Frames are made in the following manner: Two strips of board, 7 feet long, 2 or 2½ inches wide—two strips 3 feet long, 1½ inches wide, the whole ¾ of an inch thick—nail the short strips across the ends of the long ones, and it makes a frame 7 by 3 feet, which is a convenient size for all purposes. On one of the long strips nails are driven 3 inches apart, extending from the top to the bottom. After the apples are pared, they are quartered and cored, and with a needle and twine, or stout thread strung into lengths long enough to reach twice across the frame; the ends of the twine are then tied together, and the strings hung on the nails across the frame. The apples will soon dry so that the strings can be doubled on the nails, and fresh ones put on or the whole of them removed, and others put in their place. As fast as the apples become sufficiently dry they can be taken from the strings, and the same strings used to dry more on. If large apples are used to dry, they can be cut in smaller pieces. Pears and quinces and other fruits that can be strung, may be dried in this way.

To Dry Green Corn.—1. Clean the silk carefully from the corn. Put it in a steamer, over a kettle of hot water. Steam ten minutes. Then draw a knife through each row of the kernels, and scrape out the pulp, leaving the hulls on the cob. Spread on plates and dry carefully without scorching.—2. Husk the corn and silk it. Then shave it off with a sharp knife. To six quarts of the shaved corn add a teacup of sugar and stir it all up together. Put it on a pie platter and plates and set in the oven. Let it scald ten minutes; then take it out and put it on a clean table cloth, and spread in the sun and let it dry. When dry, put in a jar or box to keep.

To Dry Peaches.—Never pare peaches to dry. Let them get mellow enough to be in good eating condition, put them in boiling water for a moment or two, and the skins will come off like a charm. Let them be in the water long enough, but no longer. The gain is at least six-fold—saving of time in removing the skin, great saving of the peach, the part of the peach saved is the best part, less time to stone the peaches, less time to dry them, and better when dried. A whole bushel can be done in a boiler at once, and then the water turned off.

To Dry Currants.—Take fully ripe currants, stemmed, 5 lbs.; sugar 1 lb.; put into a brass kettle, stirring at first, then as the currants boil up to the top, skim them off; boil down the juicy syrup until quite thick and pour it over the currants, mixing well; then place on suitable dishes, and dry them by placing in a low box over which you can place a musketo-bar, to keep away flies. When properly dried, put in jars and tie paper over them. Put cold water upon them and stew as other fruit for eating or pie-making, adding more sugar if desired.

To Dry Pumpkins.—Take the ripe pumpkins, pare, cut into small pieces, stew soft, mash and strain through a colander, as if for making pies. Spread this pulp on plates in layers not quite an inch thick; dry it down in the stove oven, kept at so low a temperature as not to scorch it. In about a day it will become dry and crisp. The sheets thus made can be stowed away in a dry place, and they are always ready for use for pies or sauce. Soak the pieces over night in a little milk, and they will return to a nice pulp, as delicious as the fresh pumpkin. The quick drying after cooking prevents any portion from slightly souring as is always the case when the uncooked pieces are dried; the flavor is much better preserved, and the after cooking is saved.

To Dry Eggs.—The eggs are beaten to uniform consistency, and spread out in thin cakes on batter plates. This dries them into a paste, which is to be packed in close cans and sealed. When required for use, the paste can be dissolved in water, and beaten to a foam like fresh eggs. It is said that eggs can be preserved for years in this this way, and retain their flavor.

Apple Jelly.—Pare, core, and cut thirteen good apples into small bits: as they are cut throw them into two quarts of cold water: boil them in this, with the peel of a lemon, till the substance is extracted, and nearly half the liquor wasted; drain them through a hair sieve. And to a pint of the liquid, add one pound of loaf sugar pounded, the juice of one lemon, and the beaten whites of one or two eggs: put it into a saucepan, stir it till it boils, skim till clear, and then mould it.

Red Currant Jelly.—With three parts of fine, ripe, red currants, mix one of white currants; put them into a clean preserving pan, and stir them gently over a clear fire until the juice flows from them freely; then turn them into a fine hair sieve, and let them drain well, but without pressure. pass the juice through a folded muslin, or a jelly bag; weigh it, and then boil it fast for a quarter of an hour; add for each pound, eight ounces of sugar, coarsely powdered; stir this to it, off the fire, untill it is dissolved; give the jelly eight minutes more of quick boiling, and pour it out. It will be firm, and of excellent color and flavor. Be sure to clear off the scum as it rises, both before and after the sugar is put in, or the preserve will not be clear. Juice of red currants, three pounds; juice of white currants, one pound; fifteen minutes. Sugar, two pounds; eight minutes. An excellent jelly may be made with equal parts of the juice of red and of white currants and of raspberries, with' the same proportion of sugar and degree of boiling as mentioned in the foregoing receipt.

Black Currant Jelly.—To each pound of picked fruit, allow one gill of water; set them on the fire in the preserving pan to scald, but do not let them boil; bruise them well with a silver fork, or wooden beater,—take them off and squeeze them through a hair sieve; and to every pint of juice allow a pound of loaf or raw sugar; boil it ten minutes.

Grape Jelly.—Take some of the best black grapes, strip them from the stalks, stir them with a wooden spoon over a gentle fire till they burst; strain off the juice (without pressing) through a jelly-bag or thick muslin; weigh the juice and boil it rapidly for twenty minutes; then take it from the fire, and to each pound of juice add fourteen ounces of good sugar roughly powdered, and boil quickly for a quater of an hour, stirring it constantly, and skimming it carefully. It will be quite clear, and of a pale rose color.

Apricot Jam.—Let the fruit be just in maturity, but not over ripe. Remove the skins, then cut the apricots in halves. Crack the stones, take out the kernels, bleach them in boiling water, and pound them in a mortar. Boil the broken stones, skins, and parings, in double the quantity of water required for the jam. Reduce it in the boiling to one half of its original quantity. Then strain it through a jelly-bag. To each pound of prepared apricots put a quarter of a pint of this juice, a pound of sifted loaf sugar, and the pounded kernels. Put it on the fire, which should be brisk, and stir the whole with a wooden spoon until it is of a nice consistence, but without being very stiff, or it would have a bad flavor. Put it immediately into pots, and let these stand uncovered during twenty-four hours. Then strew a little sifted sugar over the upper surface of the jam in each pot, and tie egged paper over each pot.

Raspberry Jam.—Take 1 pound loaf-sugar to every pound of fruit; bruise them together in your preserving pan with a silver-spoon, and let them simmer gently for an hour. When cold, put them into glass jars, and lay over them a bit of paper saturated with brandy —then tie them up so as carefully to exclude the air.

MANUFACTURING SECRETS.

Currant Wine.—The currants should be fully ripe when picked; put them into a large tub, in which they should remain a day or two; then crush with the hands, unless you have a small patent wine press, in which they should not be pressed too much, or the stems will be bruised, and impart a disagreeable taste to the juice. If the hands are used, put the crushed fruit, after the juice had been poured off, in a cloth or sack and press out the remaining juice. Put the juice back into the tub after cleansing it, where it should remain about three days, until the first stages of fermentation are over, and removing once or twice a day the scum copiously arising to the top. Then put the juice in a vessel—a demijohn, keg, or barrel—of a size to suit the quantity made, and to each quart of juice add 3 ℔s. of the best yellow sugar, and soft water sufficient to make a gallon. Thus, ten quarts of juice and 30 ℔s. of sugar will give you 10 gals. of wine, and so on in proportion. Those who do not like sweet wine can reduce the quantity of sugar to two and a half, or who wish it very sweet, raise to three and a half pounds per gallon. The vessel must be full, and the bung or stopper left off until fermentation ceases, which will be in 12 or 15 days. Meanwhile, the cask must be filled up daily with currant juice left over, as fermentation throws out the impure matter. When fermentation ceases, rack the wine off carefully, either from the spiggot or by a syphon, and keep running all the time. Cleanse the cask thoroughly with boiling water, then return the wine, bung up tightly, and let it stand 4 or 5 months, when it will be fit to drink, and can be bottled if desired. All the vessels, casks, etc., should be perfectly sweet, and the whole operation should be done with an eye to cleanliness. In such event, every drop of brandy or other spirituous liquors added will detract from the flavor of the wine, and will not, in the least degree, increase its keeping qualities. Currant wine made in this way will keep for an age.

Grape Wine.—Take two quarts of grape juice, two quarts of water, four pounds of sugar. Extract the juice of the grape in any simple way; if only a few quarts are desired, we do it with a strainer and a pair of squeezers, if a larger quantity is desired, put the grapes into a cheese press made particularly clean, putting on sufficient weight to extract the juice of a full hoop of grapes, being careful that none but perfect grapes are used, perfectly ripe and free from blemish. After the first pressing put a little water with the pulp and press a second time, using the juice of the second pressing with the water to be mixed with the clear grape juice. If only a few quarts are made place the wine as soon as mixed into bottles, filling them even full and allow to stand in a warm place until it ferment, which will take about thirty-six hours usually; then remove all the scum, cool and put into a dark, cool place. If a few gallons are desired place in a keg, but the keg must be even full, and after fermentation has taken place and the scum removed, draw off and bottle, and cork tight.

Cider Wine.—Let the new cider from sour apples, (ripe, sound fruit preferred,) ferment from 1 to 3 weeks, as the weather is warm or cold. When it has attained to a lively fermentation, add to each gallon, according to its acidity, from ½ a ℔. to 2 ℔s. of white crushed sugar, and let the whole ferment until it possesses precisely the taste which it is desired should be permanent. In this condition pour out a quart of the cider and add for each gallon ¼ ounce of sulphite of lime, not sulphate. Stir the powder and cider until intimately mixed, and return the emulsion to the fermenting liquid. Agitate briskly and thoroughly for a few moments, and then let the cider settle. Fermentation will cease at once. When after a few days, the cider has become clear, draw off carefully, to avoid the sediment, and bottle. If loosely corked, which is better, it will become a sparkling cider wine, and may be kept indefinitely long.

Sherry Wine.—To 40 gallons prepared cider, add 2 gals. spirits; 3 ℔s. of raisins; 6 gals. good sherry, and ½ oz. oil bitter almonds, (dissolved in alcohol.) Let it stand 10 days, and draw it off carefully; fine it down and again rack it into another cask.

Apple Wine.—Take pure cider made from sound ripe apples as it runs from the press; put sixty pounds of common brown sugar into fifteen gallons of the cider, and let it dissolve; then put the mixture into a clean barrel, and fill the barrel up to within two gallons of being full, with clean cider; put the cask in a cool place, leaving the bung out for forty-eight hours; then put in the bung, with a small vent, until fermentation wholly ceases, and bung up tight; and in one year the wine will be fit for use. This wine requires no racking; the longer it stands upon the lees, the better.

Raisin Wine.—Raisins, 5 cwt.; water 100 gallons. Put them into a cask. Mash for a fortnight, frequently stirring, and leave the bung loose until the active fermentation ceases, then add brandy, 5 gallons. Well mix, and let it stand till fine. The quantity of raisins and brandy may be altered to suit.

Port Wine.—To 40 gallons prepared cider add 6 gals. good port wine; ten quarts wild grapes, (clusters); ½ ℔. bruised rhatany root, 3 oz. tincture of kino; 3 ℔s. loaf sugar; 2 gals. spirits. Let this stand ten days; color if too light, with tincture of rhatany, then rack it off and fine it. This should be repeated until the color is perfect and the liquid clear.

Ginger Wine.—Boil together for half an hour, 7 quarts of water, 6 pounds of sugar, 2 ounces of the best ginger, bruised, and the rind of three good-sized lemons. When lukewarm put the whole into a cask, with the juice of the lemons, and ¼ of a pound of sun raisins; add one teaspoonful of new yeast, and stir the wine every day for ten days.

Strawberry Wine.—Bruised strawberries, 12 gals.; cider, 10 gals.; water, 7 gals.; sugar, 25 ℔s. Ferment, then add of bruised orris root, bruised bitter almonds, and bruised cloves, each ½ oz.; dissolved red tartar, 6 oz.

Unfermented Wine.—Gather the grapes when well ripened. Carefully remove all decayed and unripe berries. Mixed varieties, or any one of the favorite varieties of grapes may be used. Press out the juce and boil as long as any scum rises. Skim carefully from time to time. Do not boil to exceed an hour. Bottle while hot, and seal either in glass bottles, jugs, or air-tight casks. It is fit for use at any time, but after being opened it must not be allowed to ferment. Excepting strawberry syrup, this will be found the most delightful and exhilarating of all unfermented beverages. It needs no sugar, and may be reduced when drank.

Coloring for Wines.—White sugar, 1 ℔.; water, 1 gal.; put into an iron kettle, let boil, and burn to a red black, and thick; remove from the fire and add a little hot water to keep it from hardening as it cools; then bottle for use.

To Flavor Wine.—When the vinous fermentation is about half over, the flavoring ingredients are to be put into the vat and well stirred into the contents. If almonds form a component part, they are first to be beaten to a paste and mixed with a pint or two of the must. Nutmegs, cinnamon, ginger, seeds, etc., should, before they are put into the vat, be reduced to powder, and mixed with some of the must.

To Mellow Wine.—Wine either in bottle or wood, will mellow much quicker when only covered with pieces of bladder well secured, than with corks or bungs. The bladder allows the watery particles to escape, but is impervious to alcohol.

To Make Wine Settle Well.—Take a pint of wheat and boil it in a quart of water till it bursts and becomes soft; then squeeze through a linen cloth, and put a pint of the liquor into a hogshead of unsettled white wine; stir it well about, and it will become fine.

Champagne Cider.—Champagne cider is made as follows: —To 100 gals. of good cider put 3 gals. of strained honey, or 24 lbs. of good white sugar. Stir well and set it aside for a week. Clarify the cider with half a gallon of skimmed milk, or ¼ lb. of dissolved isinglass, and add 4 gals. of pure spirits. After 2 or 3 days bottle the clear cider, and it will become sparkling. In order to produce a slow fermentation, the casks containing the fermenting liquor must be bunged up tight. It is a great object to retain much of the carbonic gas in the cider, so as to develop itself after being bottled.

French Cider.—After the fruit is mashed in a mill, between iron cylinders, it is allowed to remain in a large tun or tub for 14 or 15 hours, before pressing. The juice is placed in casks, which are kept quite full, and so placed upon gawntrees, or stillions, that small tubs may be put under them, to receive the matter that works over. At the end of 3 or 4 days for sweet cider, and 9 or 10 days for strong cider, it is racked into sulphured casks, and then stored in a cool place.

Western Cider.—To one pound of sugar, add one half an ounce of tartaric acid, and two tablespoonfuls of good yeast. Dissolve the sugar in one quart of warm water; put all in a gallon jug; shake it well, fill the jug with pure cold water, let it stand uncorked twelve hours, and it is fit for use.

Cider without Apples.—To each gallon of cold water, put 1 lb. common sugar, ½ oz. tartaric acid, 1 tablespoonful of yeast, shake well, make in the evening, and it will be fit for use next day. Make in a keg a few gallons at a time, leaving a few quarts to make into next time; not using yeast again until the keg needs rinsing. If it gets a little sour make a little more into it, or put as much water with it as there is cider, and put it with the vinegar. If it is desired to bottle this cider by manufacturers of small drinks, you will proceed as follows: Put in a barrel 5 gallons hot water, 30 lbs. brown sugar, ¾ lb. tartaric acid, 25 gallons cold water, 3 pints of hop or brewer's yeast worked into paste with ¾ lb. flour, and 1 pint water will be required in making this paste, put altogether in a barrel, which it will fill, and let it work 24 hours

—the yeast running out at a bung all the time, by putting in a little occasionally to keep it full. Then bottle, putting in 2 or 3 broken raisins to each bottle, and it will nearly equal champagne.

To clear Cider.—To clear and improve cider generally, take two quarts of ground horseradish and one pound of thick gray filtering paper to the barrel, and either shake or stir until the paper has separated into small shreds, and let it stand for twenty-four hours, when the cider may be drawn off by means of a syphon or a stop cock. Instead of paper a preparation of wool may be taken, which is to be had in the market here, and which is preferable to paper, as it has simply to be washed with water when it may be used again.

To keep Cider Sweet and Sweeten when sour.— To keep cider perfect, take a keg and bore holes in the bottom of it; spread a piece of woolen cloth at the bottom; then fill with clean sand closely packed; draw your cider from a barrel just as fast as it will run through the sand; after this, put it in clean barrels which have had a piece of cotton or linen cloth 2 by 7 inches dipped in melted sulphur and burned inside of them, thereby absorbing the sulphur fumes (this process will also sweeten sour cider); then keep it in a cellar or room where there is no fire, and add ½ ℔. white mustard seed to each barrel. If cider is long made, or souring when you get it, about 1 qt. of hickory ashes (or a little more of other hard wood ashes) stirred into each barrel will sweeten and clarify it nearly equal to rectifying it as above; but if it is not rectified, it must be racked off to get clear of the pomace, as, with this in it, it will sour. Oil or whisky barrels are best to put cider in, or ½ pint sweet oil to a barrel, or a gallon of whisky to a barrel, or both, may be added with decidedly good effects; isinglass, 4 oz. to each barrel, helps to clarify and settle cider that is not going to be rectified.

Brandy.—To 40 gals. of pure or neutral spirits, add 1 ℔. crude tartar, dissolved in 1 gal. hot water; acetic ether, ¼ pint; bruised raisins, 6 ℔s.; tinct. kino, 2 ounces; sugar, 3 ℔s.; color with sugar coloring. Stand 14 days, and draw off.

British Brandy.—Clean spirits, 100 gals.; nitric ether, 2 ℔s.; cassia buds (ground), ½ ℔.; bitter almond meal, ½ ℔.; orris root (sliced), 6 ounces; powdered cloves, one ounce; capsicum, 1 oz.; good vinegar, 2 gals.; brandy coloring, 1 quart. Mix well in an empty cognac cask, and let them macerate for a fortnight, occasionally stirring. The proportion of the ingredients may be varied by the skillful brewer, as much depends on their respective strengths.

Cognac Brandy.—To every 10 gals. of pure spirits add 2 quarts New England rum, or 1 quart Jamaica rum, and from 30 to 40 drops of oil cognac cut in half a pint of alcohol, and color with burnt sugar to suit.

French Brandy.—Pure spirits, 1 gal.; best French brandy, or any kind you wish to imitate, 1 quart; loaf sugar, 2 ounces; sweet spirits of nitre, ½ ounce; a few drops of tinct. of catechu, or oak bark, to roughen the taste if desired, and color to suit.

Pale Brandy.—Is made the same as by the above receipt, using pale instead of the French, and using only 1 oz. tinct. of kino for every 5 gals.

Cherry Brandy.—To every 10 gals. of brandy made by the receipt for French brandy, add 3 quarts of wild black cherries, stones and all bruised; crushed sugar, 2 ℔s.; let it stand for one week, then draw or rack it off as it is wanted for use.

Gin.—Take 100 gallons of clean, rectified spirits; add, after you have killed the oils well, 1½ oz. of the oil of English juniper, ½ ounce of angelica essence, ½ oz. of the oil bitter almonds, ½ oz. of the oil of coriander, and ½ oz. of the oil of caraway; put this into the rectified spirit and well rummage it up: this is what the rectifiers call strong gin. To make this up, as it is called by the trade, add 45 ℔s. of loaf-sugar, dissolved; then rummage the whole well up together with 4 oz. of roch alum. For finings, there may be added 2 oz. of salts of tartar.

Holland Gin.—To 40 gals. of neutral spirits, add 2 ounces spirits nitre; 4 ℔s. of loaf sugar; one oz. oil juiper; ⅛ ounce oil caraway. The juniper and caraway to be first cut in a quart of alcohol; stand 24 hours.

English Gin.—Plain malt spirit, 100 gals.; spirits of turpentine, 1 pint; bay salt, 7 ℔s. Mix and distill. The difference in the flavor of gin is produced by varying the proportion of turpentine, and by occassionally adding a small quantity of juniper berries.

Cordial Gin.—Of the oil of bitter almonds, vitriol, turpentine, and juniper, ½ a drachm each, kill the oils in spirits of wine; 15 gallons of clean rectified proof-spirits, to which add 1 drachm of coriander seeds, 1 drachm of pulverized orris root, ½ pint of elder-flower water, with 10 ℔s. of sugar and 5 gals. of water or liquor.

To Imitate Schiedam Schnapps.—To 25 gals good common gin, 5 over proof, add 15 pints strained honey; 2 gals. clear water; 5 pints white-sugar syrup; 5 pints spirit of nutmegs mixed with the nitric ether; 5 pints orange-flower water; 7 quarts pure water; 1 ounce acetic ether; 8 drops oil of wintergreen, dissolved with the acetic ether. Mix all the ingredients well; if necessary, fine with alum and salt of tartar.

Irish or Scotch Whisky.—To 40 gallons proof spirits add 60 drops of creosote, dissolved in 1 quart of alcohol; 2 ounces acetic acid; 1 pound loaf sugar. Stand 48 hours.

Monongahela Whisky.—To 40 gallons proof spirits, add 2 ounces spirits of nitre; 4 pounds dried peaches; 4 pounds N. O. sugar; 1 quart rye (burnt and ground like coffee); ¼ pound allspice; ½ pound cinnamon; ½ pound cloves. Put in the ingredients, and after standing 5 days, draw it off, and strain the same, if necessary.

Bourbon Whisky.—To 100 gallons pure proof spirits, add 4 ounces pear oil; 2 oz. pelarganic ether; 13 drs. oil of wintergreen, dissolved in the ether; 1 gallon wine vinegar. Color with burnt sugar.

To Neutralize Whisky, to make Various Liquors. —To 40 gallons of whisky, add 1 ½ ℔s. unslaked lime, ¾ ℔. alum, and ½ pint spirits of nitre. Stand 24 hours and draw it off.

Jamaica Rum.—To 24 gallons New-England rum, add 5 gallons Jamaica rum; 2 oz. butyric ether; ½ ounce oil of caraway, cut with alcohol, 95 per cent. Color with sugar coloring.

Santa Cruz Rum.—To 50 gallons pure proof spirits, add 5 gallons Santa Cruz rum; 5 pounds refined sugar, in ½ gallon of water; 3 ounces butyric acid; 2 ounces acetic ether. Color if necessary.

Pine Apple Rum.—To 50 gallons rum, made by the fruit method, add 25 pine-apples sliced, and 8 pounds white sugar. Let it stand two weeks before drawing off.

Stomach Bitters.—European Gentian root, 1 ½ ounce; orange peel, 2 ½ ounces; cinnamon, ¼ ounce; anise seed, ½ ounce; coriander seed, ½ ounce; cardamom seed, ⅛ ounce; unground Peruvian bark, ½ ounce; gum kino, ¼ ounce; bruise all these articles, and put them into the best alcohol, 1 pint; let it stand a week and pour off the clear tincture; then boil the dregs a few minutes in 1 quart of water, strain, and press out all the strength; now dissolve loaf sugar, 1 pound in the hot liquid, adding 3 quarts cold water, and mix with spirit tincture first poured off, or you can add these, and let it stand on the dregs if preferred.

Brandy Bitters.—Bruised gentian, 8 ounces; orange peel, 5 ounces; cardamoms, 3 ounces; cassia, 1 ounce; cochineal, ¼ ounce; spirit 1 gallon. Digest for one week, then decant the clear, and pour on the dregs, water, 5 pints. Digest for one week longer, decant, and mix the two tinctures together.

Home Brewed Ale.—For this purpose a quarter of malt, (8 bus.) is obtained at the malt house—or, if wished to be extra strong, nine bushels of malt are taken, with hops, 12 ℔s.; yeast, 5 qts. The malt being crushed or ground, is mixed with 72 gals. of water at the temperature of 160°, and covered up for 3 hours, when 40 gallons are drawn off, into which the hops are put, and left to infuse. Sixty gallons of water at a temperatue of 170° are then added to the malt in the mash-tub, and well mixed, and after standing 2 hours, sixty gallons are drawn off. The wort from these two mashes is boiled with the hops for 2 hours, and after being cooled down to 65°, is strained through a flannel bag into a fermenting-tub, where it is mixed with the yeast and left to work for 24 or 30 hours. It is then run into barrels to cleanse, a few gallons being reserved for filling up the casks as the yeast works over.

Cheap Beer.—1. Water 15 gals.; boil half the water with ¼ ℔. hops; then add to the other half in the tun, and well mix with 1 gal. molasses and a little yeast.—2. Fill a boiler with the green shells of peas, pour on water till it rises half an inch above the shells, and simmer for three hours. Strain off the liquor, and add a strong decoction of the wood sage, or the hop, so as to render it pleasantly bitter, then ferment in the usual manner. The wood sage is the best substitute for hops, and being free from any anodyne property is entitled to a preference. By boiling a fresh quantity of shells in the decoction before it becomes cold, it may be so thoroughly impregnated with saccharine matter, as to afford a liquor, when fermented, as strong as ale.

Hop Beer.—Turn 5 quarts of water on 6 ounces of hops; boil three hours; strain off the liquor; turn on 4 quarts more of water, and 12 spoonfuls of ginger, and boil the hops 3 hours longer; strain and mix it with the other liquor, and stir in 2 quarts of molasses. Brown, very dry, half pound of bread, and put in—rusked bread is best. Pound it fine, and brown it in a pot, like coffee. After cooling to be about lukewarm, add a pint of new yeast that is free from salt. Keep the beer covered, in a temperate situation, till fermentation has ceased, which is known by the settling of the froth; then turn it into a keg or bottles, and keep it in a cool place.

Philadelphia Beer.—Water 30 gallons; brown sugar 20 ℔s.; ginger, bruised, 1¼ ℔.; cream of tartar ¼ ℔.; supercarbonate of soda 3 oz.; oil of lemon, cut in a little alcohol, 1 teaspoon; whites of 10 eggs, well beaten; hops 2 oz.; yeast 1 quart. The ginger root and hops should be boiled 20 or 30 minutes in enough of the water to make all milk warm, then strained into the rest, and the yeast added and allowed to work over night; skimmed and bottled.

Sassafras Beer.—Have ready 2 gals. of soft water; one quart of wheat bran; a large handful of dried apples; half a pint of molasses; a small handful of hops; half a pint of strong fresh yeast, and a piece of sassafras root the size of an egg. Put all the ingredients (save molasses and yeast) at once in a large kettle. Boil until the apples are quite soft. Pour the molasses in a small, clean tub or a large pan. Set a hair sieve over the vessel and strain the mixture through it. Let it stand until it becomes only milk warm, when, stir in the yeast, put the liquor immediately into the keg or jugs, and let it stand, uncorked, to ferment. Fill the jugs quite full, that the liquor in fermentation may run over. Set them in a large tub. When the fermentation has subsided, cork and use next day. 2 large tablespoons of ginger stirred into the molasses, will be found to be an improvement. If the yeast is stirred in while the liquor is too warm, it will be apt to turn sour. If the liquor is not at once put into jugs, it will not ferment well. Keep in a cool place. This beer is only for present use, as it will not keep more than 2 days in very warm weather.

Spruce Beer.—1. Boil a handful of hops, and 2 of the chips of sassafras root, in 10 gallons of water; strain it, and turn on, while hot, a gallon of molasses, 2 spoonfuls of the essence of spruce, 2 spoonfuls of ginger, and 1 of pounded allspice. Put it into a cask; and when cold enough, add half a pint of good yeast; stir it well; stop it close; when clear, bottle and cork it.—2. For 3 gals. water put in 1 qt. and ½ pint of molasses, 3 eggs well beaten, yeast 1 gill. Into 2 qts. of the water boiling hot put 50 drops of any oil you wish the flavor of; or mix 1 oz. each, oils sassafras, spruce and wintergreen, then use 50 drops of the mixed oils.

Molasses Beer.—Hops 1 oz.; water 1 gal.; boil for 10 minutes, strain, add molasses 1 ℔.; and when lukewarm, yeast 1 spoonful. Ferment.

Root Beer.—Take 3 gals. of molasses; add 10 gals. of water at 60° Fah. Let this stand two hours, then pour into a barrel, and add powdered or bruised sassafras and wintergreen bark, each ½ ℔., bruised sarsaparilla root ½ ℔., yeast one pint, water enough to fill the barrel, say 25 gals. Ferment for 12 hours and bottle.

Ginger Beer Powders.—Take 2 drs. of fine loaf sugar, 8 grs. of ginger, 26 grs. of carbonate of potassa, all in fine powder; mix them intimately in a Wedgwood's ware mortar. Take also 27 grs. of citric or tartaric acid (the first is the pleasantest, but the last is the cheapest). The acid is to be kept separate from the mixture. The beer is prepared from the powders thus: Take two tumbler-glasses, each half filled with water; stir up the compound powder in one of them, and the acid powder in another, then mix the two liquors; an effervescence takes place, the beer is prepared, and may be drunk off.

Spruce Beer Powders.—White sugar, 1 drachm; bicarbonate of soda, 1 scruple; essence of spruce, 8 grains; essence of lemon, 1 grain. Mix and wrap it in blue paper. Then add tartaric acid, ½ drachm, and wrap it in white paper. For use: dissolve each paper in separate glasses, one third full of water, pour one into the other, and drink immediately.

To Restore Beer when Musty.—Run it through some hops that have been boiled in strong wort, and afterwards work it with double the quantity of new malt liquor; or if the fault is in the cask, draw it off into a sweet cask, and having boiled ½ ℔. of brown sugar in 1 quart of water, add 1 or 2 spoonfuls of yeast before it is quite cold, and when the mixture ferments, pour it into the cask.

Sham Champagnes.—Take 1 lemon, sliced; 1 tablespoonful of tartaric acid; 1 ounce of race ginger; 1½ ounce of sugar; 2½ gallons of boiling water poured on the above. When blood warm, add 1 gill of distillery yeast, or 2 gills of home-brewed. Let it stand in the sun through the day. When cold, in the evening, bottle, cork, and wire it. In two days it is ready for use.

American Champagne.—Good cider (crab-apple cider is the best), 7 gals.; best fourth-proof brandy, 1 quart; genuine champagne wine 5 quarts; milk, 1 gal.; bitartrate of potassa, 2 ounces. Mix, and let stand a short time; bottle while fermenting. An excellent imitation.

Cider Champagne.—Good cider, 20 gals.; spirit, 1 gal.; honey or sugar, 6 ℔s. Mix, and let them rest for a fortnight; then fine with skimmed milk, 1 quart. This, put up in champagne bottles, silvered, and labeled, has often been sold for champagne. It opens very sparkling.

Coloring for Liquors.—Take 2 pounds crushed or lump sugar, put it into a kettle that will hold 4 to 6 quarts, with ½ tumbler of water. Boil it untill it is black, then take it off and cool with water, stirring it as you put in the water.

Ginger Pop.—Crushed white sugar 28 ℔s., water 30 gal., yeast 1 pint, powdered ginger (best) 1 ℔., essence of lemon ½ oz.; essence of cloves ¼ oz. To the ginger pour half a gallon of boiling water and let it stand 15 or 20 minutes. Dissolve the sugar in 2 gals. of warm water, pour both into a barrel half filled with cold water, then add the essence and the yeast; let it stand half an hour, then fill up with cold water. Let it ferment 6 to 12 hours, and bottle.

Portable Lemonade.—Mix strained lemon juice with loaf sugar, in the proportion of 4 large lemons to a pound, or as much as it will hold in solution; grate the rind of the lemons into this, and preserve the mixture in a jar. If this is to sweet, add a little citric acid. Use a tablespoonful to a tumbler of water.

Citron Cordial.—Yellow rind of citrons, 3 ℔s.; orange peel, 1 ℔.; nutmegs bruised 2 oz.; proof spirits 13 gallons; distill or macerate, add water sufficient, and 2 ℔s. of fine lump sugar for every gallon of the cordial.

Strawberry or Raspberry Cordial.—Sugar down the berries overnight, using more sugar than you would for the table, about half as much again. In the morning lay them in a hair sieve over the basin; let them remain until evening, so as to thoroughly drain; then put the juice in a thick flannel bag; let it drain all night, being careful not to squeeze it, as that takes out the brightness and clearness. All this should be done in a cool cellar, or it will be apt to sour. Add brandy in proportion of one-third the quantity of the juice, and as much more sugar as the taste demands. Bottle it tightly. It will keep six or eight years, and is better at last than at first.

Clove Cordial.—Bruised cloves 1 oz., or essential oil 1 dr., to every 4 gallons of proof spirits. If distilled it should be drawn over with a pretty quick fire. It is preferred of a very deep color, and is therefore strongly colored with poppy-flowers or cochineal, or more commonly with brandy coloring, or red sanders wood. It should have 3 ℔s. of sugar to the gallon, and this need not be very fine. The addition of 1 drachm of bruised pimento, or 5 drops of the oil for every ounce of cloves, improves this cordial.

Ginger Cordial.—Pick one pound of large white currants from their stalks, lay them in a basin, and strew over them the rind of an orange and a lemon cut very thin, or half a teaspoonful of essence of lemon, and one ounce and a half of the best ground ginger and a quart of good whisky. Let all lie for twenty-four hours. If it tastes strong of the ginger, then strain it; if not, let it lie for twelve hours longer. To every quart of strained juice add one pound of loaf sugar pounded; when the sugar is quite dissolved and the liquor appears clear, bottle it. This cordial is also extremely good made with raspberries instead of currants.

Coriander Cordial.—1 ℔. of coriander seeds; 1 oz. of caraways, and the peel and juice of 1 orange to every 3 gallons of proof spirits.

Cooling Drinks for Hot Weather.—A delicious and slightly aperient effervescing citrate of magnesia may be made by thoroughly mixing 3 ounces of powdered loaf sugar with 2 ounces of powdered citric acid, then add ¾ ounce of calcined magnesia. 1½ ounce of bicarbonate of soda, and 1½ ounce of tartaric acid. Pass the whole thrice through a sieve, and then moisten it with very strong alcohol. Granulate it by passing it through a coarse sieve, and dry on a wooden tray at a temperature of 50° C. When dry add ten drops essential oil of lemons, and then bottle at once in clean dry bottles.

Lemon Syrup.—Coffee sugar, 3 ℔s.; water, 1½ pints; dissolve by gentle heat, and add critic acid 3 oz., and flavor with oil or extract of lemon. Or take citric acid in powder ¼ oz.; oil of lemon 4 drops; simple syrup 1 quart. Rub the acid and oil in 3 or 4 spoons of the syrup, then add the mixture to the remainder, and dissolve with gentle heat.

Effervescing Lemonade.—Take powdered white sugar, 1 pound; bicarbonate of soda, ¼ pound; essence of lemon, 1½ drs. Mix and divide it into six dozen papers. Tartaric or citric acid, 5 ounces. Divided into the same number of papers. The granulated effervescent powders found in the market are made in the following way:—A clean iron or copper pan is heated over a slow fire, and the mixture finely pulverized sugar and citric acid put in and well stirred, until it commences to cake, without of course changing its color; the pan is then taken from the fire and the bicarbonate of soda stirred into the mixture, until it is uniformly distributed through the mass, when the whole is pressed through a coarse sieve, and the granules exposed to the air for a little while to harden. They are then ready for bottling. A tablespoonful of this put in a glass of water will dissolve almost instantaneously, producing a good lemonade.

Mead.—The following is a good receipt for mead:—On twenty pounds of honey pour five gallons of boiling water; boil, and remove the scum as it rises; add one ounce of best hops, and boil for ten minutes; then put the liquor into a tub to cool; when all but cold add a little yeast spread upon a slice of toasted bread; let it stand in a warm room. When fermentation is finished, bung it down, leaving a peg-hole which can afterward be closed, and in less than a year it will be fit to bottle.

Blackberry Wine.—Gather the berries when perfectly ripe, and in such a manner, as to avoid bruising. Empty them, as fast as gathered, into a tub until you have a quantity sufficient to fill, with juice, the cask in which you propose to make the wine. Have the utensils, etc., required in the process, all ready before you pick—or at least before you mash your berries. Everything must be scrupulously clean. You want a keg, a beater of seasoned hard wood, a pail, a large bowl, tureen or other vessel into which to strain your juice, a good thick strainer—two or three folds of fine white flannel is the best material—a couple of yards of osnaburgs, a spare tub or a bucket or two, and a tub of soft spring water. Everything must be perfectly clean and free from dirt or odor of any kind. Crush the berries thoroughly with the beater, and then after straining the liquor, which runs freely from the pulp through the folded flannel, empty it into the cask, measuring it as you put it in. When the juice has been all drained from the pulp, you proceed to press the pulp dry. If the quantity is large, this had best be done by a regular press, but if only a few gallons are wanted, the osnaburg answers very well. Stretch out the osnaburg, put a gallon or a gallon and a half of the pulp into the centre, fold the cloth over it on each side, and let a strong hand at either end twist the cloth with all their strength; when the juice is well pressed out, remove and lay aside the cake of pomace, and put in more pulp. This process is apparently rough, but is both rapid and effectual. The juice so extracted is strained and measured into the cask as before mentioned. The flannel strainer and the osnaburg may need rinsing occasionally during the work. When all the pulp is pressed, put the hard cakes of pomace taken from the cloth into a tub, and pour upon them a little more soft spring water than you have clear juice; break up the balls and wash them thoroughly in the water, so as to obtain all the juice left in the mass, and then strain it clear: measure out as many gallons of this water as you have of clear juice, say five gallons of the water to five gallons of the juice, dissolve in each gallon of the water six pounds of sugar (brown or white, as you want a common or first-rate wine) and when thoroughly dissolved, add the juice (first passing it again through the strainer), and mix them. Then rinse out your cask, put it where it can stand undisturbed in a cellar; fill it perfectly full of the mixture, and lay a cloth loosely over the bung-hole. In two or three days fermentation will commence, and impurities run over at the bung; look at it every day, and if it does not run over, with some of the mixture which you have reserved in another vessel, fill it up to the bung. In about three weeks fermentation will have ceased, and the wine be still; fill it again, drive in the bung tight, nail a tin over it, and let it remain undisturbed until the following November, or what is better, March. Then draw it off, without shaking the cask, put it into bottles or demijohns, cork tightly and seal over. For a ten-gallon cask, you will need about 4⅓ gallons of juice, 4⅓ gallons of water, and 26 pounds of sugar, and in the same proportion for larger or smaller quantities. Some persons add spirit to the wine, but instead of doing good, it is only an injury. Another process is, after pouring in the mixture for a ten-gallon cask, to beat up the whites of two or three eggs into a froth, put them into the cask, and with a long stick mix them thoroughly with the wine. In five or six days, draw the now clarified wine off by a spigot, and without shaking the cask at all, into a clean cask, bung up and tin, to be drawn off into glass in November or March. The more carefully your juice is strained, the better the quality of your sugar, and the more scrupulously clean your utensils, particularly your kegs, are, the purer and better will be your wine. The best quality, when you gather your own fruit, and make it yourself, cost you only the price of the white sugar, and when bottled will cost you in money about twelve and a half cents a bottle.

Sherbet.—Boil in 3 pints of water 6 or 8 stalks of green rhubarb, and 4 oz. of raisins or figs; when the water has boiled about half an hour, strain it, and mix it with a teaspoonful of rose water, and orange or lemon syrup to the taste. Drink it cold.

Lemon Sherbet.—Dissolve 1½ ℔s. of loaf sugar in 1 quart of water; add the juice of 10 lemons; press the lemons so as to extract both the juice and the oil of the rind, and let the peel remain a while in the water and sugar. Strain through a sieve and freeze like ice cream.

Orange Sherbet.—Take the juice of 1 dozen oranges, and pour 1 pint of boiling water on the peel, and let it stand, covered, half an hour. Boil 1 ℔. of loaf sugar in 1 pint of water, skim, and then add the juice and the water from the peel to the sugar. Strain and cool, or freeze it. The juice of 2, and a little more sugar improves it.

Persian Sherbet.—Pulverized sugar 1 ℔.; super carbonate of soda 4 ounces; tartaric acid 3 oz.; put all the articles into the stove oven when moderately warm, being separate upon paper or plates; let them remain sufficiently long to dry out all dampness absorbed from the air, then rub about 40 drops of lemon oil, (or if preferred any other flavored oil,) thoroughly with the sugar in a mortar—wedge-wood is the best—then add the soda and acid, and continue the rubbing until all are thoroughly mixed.

Wax Putty, for Leaky Casks, Bungs, etc.—Spirits turpentine, 2 pounds; tallow, 4 pounds; yellow wax 8 pounds; solid turpentine 12 pounds. Melt the wax and solid turpentine together over a slow fire; then add the tallow. When melted, remove far from the fire; then stir in the spirits turpentine, and let it cool.

Raspberry Syrup.—Take orris root bruised, any quantity, say ½ ℔., and just handsomely cover it with dilute alcohol, (76 per cent, alcohol, and water, equal quantities,) so that it cannot be made any stronger of the root.

Soda Syrup.—The common or more watery syrups are made by using loaf or crushed sugar, 8 pounds; pure water 1 gallon; gum arabic, 2 ounces; mix in a brass or copper kettle; boil until the gum is dissolved, then skim and strain through white flannel, after which add tartaric acid, 5½ ounces, dissolved in hot water; to flavor, use extract of lemon, orange, rose, pineapple, peach, sarsaparilla, strawberry, etc., ½ ounce to each bottle, or to your taste.